P9-BYD-478
201016659
793.3 GAR
Irish step dancing

DANCE

Irish Step Dancing

by Wendy Garofoli

Consultant: Rachel R. Knutson
Teacher and Director, Shamrock School of Irish Step Dance
Apple Valley, Minnesota

Capstone

Mankato, Minnesota

Snap Books are published by Capstone Press,
151 Good Counsel Drive, P.O. Box 669, Mankato, Minnesota 56002.
www.capstonepress.com

Printed in the United States of America

Library of Congress Cataloging-in-Publication Data
Garofoli, Wendy.
Irish step dancing / by Wendy Garofoli.
p. cm. — (Snap books. Dance)
Summary: "Describes Irish step dancing, including history and basic steps" — Provided by publisher.
Includes bibliographical references and index.
ISBN-13: 978-1-4296-1351-4 (hardcover)
ISBN-10: 1-4296-1351-3 (hardcover)
1. Step dancing — Juvenile literature. 2. Folk dancing, Irish — Juvenile literature. I. Title. II. Series.
GV1793.G37 2008
793.3'1 — dc22 2007034766

Editor: Jennifer Besel

Designer: Veronica Bianchini

Photo Researcher: Jo Miller

Photo Credits: All photos by Capstone Press/Karon Dubke, except:
Alamy/Lebrecht Music and Arts Photo Library, 7
Corbis/Robbie Jack, 4–5
Courtesy of the author Wendy Garofoli, 32
PhotoEdit Inc./Kayte M. Deioma, 27

Acknowledgements:
Capstone Press would like to thank Cormac and Natalie O'Shea and the dancers at O'Shea Irish Dance for their assistance preparing this book.

1 2 3 4 5 6 13 12 11 10 09 08

Table of Contents

Chapter One

Irish Dance at a Glance

Furiously flying feet.
Still, straight arms.

It's Irish step, and it's a dance that has audiences around the world hooked.

Are you ready to get hooked on Irish step too? Irish step has a rich history. And that history is deeply connected to the way the dance is performed today.

Irish Roots

Irish step is a folk dance that began with the ancient Gaels who settled in Ireland more than 2,000 years ago. But passing on the tradition of dance wasn't always easy. For hundreds of years, England controlled Ireland. English laws forced the Irish to hide their traditions. But around 1750, Irish step dancers, called dance masters, began traveling to different counties. They taught villagers dance steps and competed against other dancers. These competitions were called feiseanna (FESH-ah-na).

In the 1800s, England finally granted the Irish freedom to practice their culture. Organizations such as the Gaelic League and the Irish Dancing Commission were formed. The groups created strict rules for teaching, judging, and competing. These organizations continue today and work to preserve the heritage of Irish dance.

Chapter Two

Getting Started

Don't worry. You don't have to be Irish to Irish step dance.

Schools across the United States are devoted to teaching this style. Studios offer lessons for both boys and girls. You can also find workshops, dance festivals, and classes through local Irish cultural centers. Even instructional videos can teach you an Irish step or two. But before you enter your first Irish step dance class, you'll need to get the right stuff to wear.

Curly Competitors

If you're getting ready to perform at a feis (FESH), be prepared to break out the curlers. Curly hair is a big part of a girl's costume. Before competitions, girls sit for hours while their hair is rolled in curlers. Some have at least 100 curlers put on their heads! They even sleep with them in to get the best curls possible. But if sleeping in curlers isn't for you, don't stop dancing. You can buy a curly wig!

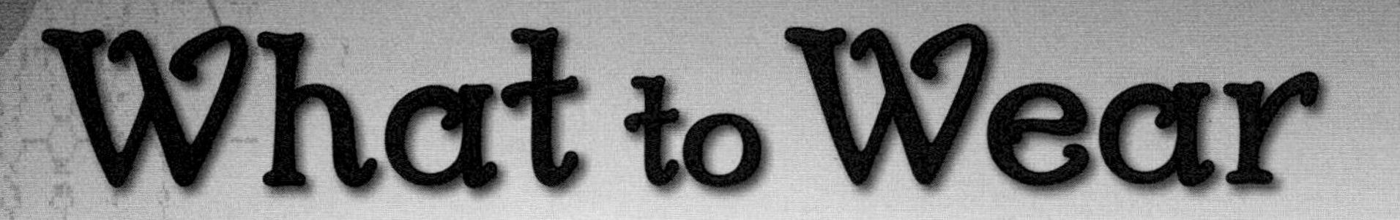

What to Wear

No need for leotards here. Shorts and a T-shirt will be just fine for practice. Girls will also practice wearing poodle socks. These tall socks are worn in performances too.

For feiseanna, the outfits are much fancier. Girls wear dresses that are copies of traditional Irish peasant dresses. These dresses are decorated with Celtic designs. For boys, a kilt or pants paired with a dress shirt is just the thing.

Fabulous Feet

Shoes are an important part of Irish step. You'll need two types of shoes: soft shoes and hard shoes. For girls, soft shoes look like black ballet shoes with fancy lacing. Girls soft shoes can also be called pumps or ghillies. Soft shoes for boys actually have a hard heel.

Hard shoes are a lot like tap shoes. For hard shoe dances, both boys and girls wear shoes that have a fiberglass tap on the toe and heel.

Chapter Three

Different Dances

Irish dancing requires grace and light-footed stepping.

As part of the style, dancers' arms remain flat at their sides. Instead, the legs and feet do most of the work. Feet should be pointed when they lift off the ground.

You'll find that the body position is much the same for each kind of Irish dance. It's the steps that change. The foot movements in Irish step change according to what music is being played.

There are many different Irish step dances. You've probably heard of the jig before. But dances like the hornpipe, the reel, and set dances are also part of Irish step. Music and footwork make each dance unique.

The Jig

The origin of the jig is unknown. Some people think it came from Italian music, while others believe the original dance masters came up with the jig. Wherever it came from, the jig stands out from other styles because of its quick, steady rhythm.

The jig does have a few variations. The single jig is danced in soft shoes and has light, elegant leg lifts. The treble jig is a bit more complicated. You do more kicking and stomping in the treble jig.

Toe-Tapping Tunes

Live music is a key part of the feis. Musicians play Irish instruments, such as the fiddle, accordion, and bagpipes. For dancers, live music is more challenging than recorded music. Musicians might play faster or slower than you expect. Listen closely to the music, and you'll be able to keep the beat.

The Reel

The reel was originally a Scottish dance developed around 1750. But Irish dance masters learned this style and made it their own. The reel is faster than the jig. Both boys and girls dance the reel, but their styles are slightly different. For girls, it's a light, quick soft-shoe dance that has lots of leaping. Boys get to bang and click their heels more.

The Hornpipe

The hornpipe is more advanced than the jig or reel. While most reels and jigs are performed in soft shoes, the hornpipe requires hard tap shoes. The hornpipe has a slightly slower tempo than the reel.

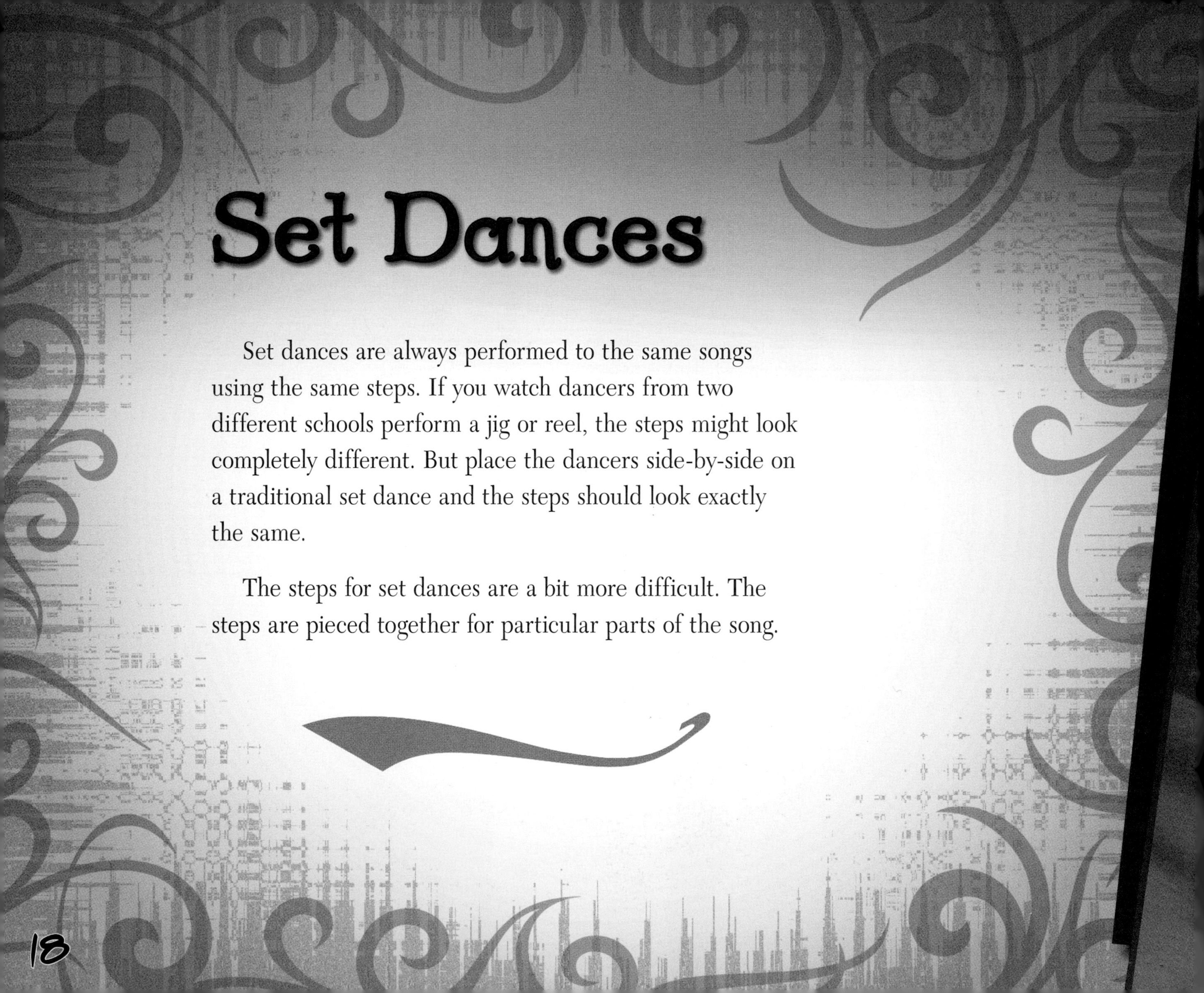

Set Dances

Set dances are always performed to the same songs using the same steps. If you watch dancers from two different schools perform a jig or reel, the steps might look completely different. But place the dancers side-by-side on a traditional set dance and the steps should look exactly the same.

The steps for set dances are a bit more difficult. The steps are pieced together for particular parts of the song.

Chapter four

Let's Dance

Now let's lace up those ghillies and start moving!

Beginning Irish dancers learn reel and jig steps, which are performed in soft shoes. To start, you must learn the basic position. Begin with the heel of your right foot touching the tips of the toes on your left. Your right foot should be turned out, with your left knee tucked directly behind your right.

Jump Threes

Now you are ready to learn the jump threes. Starting in the basic position, lift your right foot, keeping the knee straight and the toes pointed. Jump up and kick your left foot back to your behind. Land on your right foot, then step forward with your left. You should end up in the basic position.

Hop Threes

Next you can learn the hop threes. Again, start in the basic position. Hop on your left foot as high as you can and land back on that foot. At the same time, lift your right foot across your left knee. You should try to touch your left hip with your right foot. When you land, step slightly forward on your right foot, and tuck the left foot behind in the basic position.

Sevens

The side step, or sevens, is a basic Irish step used for traveling. From basic position, hop in the direction of your front foot. If your right foot is forward, hop to the right with that foot. Next, your left foot steps in the same direction, but stays behind your right foot. Repeat these steps two more times.

Scissors

Irish dance is an art form that's always changing. Teachers may add new steps to increase difficulty and showmanship. One newer and harder step is called scissors. Starting in the basic position with your right foot in front, jump in the air and point your toes. As you are in midair, switch your feet from back to front again. Do this by swinging your right leg behind and then swinging it back to the front before landing back in the starting position. Make sure your legs stay absolutely straight. Try to move your legs from the hip and not just from the feet.

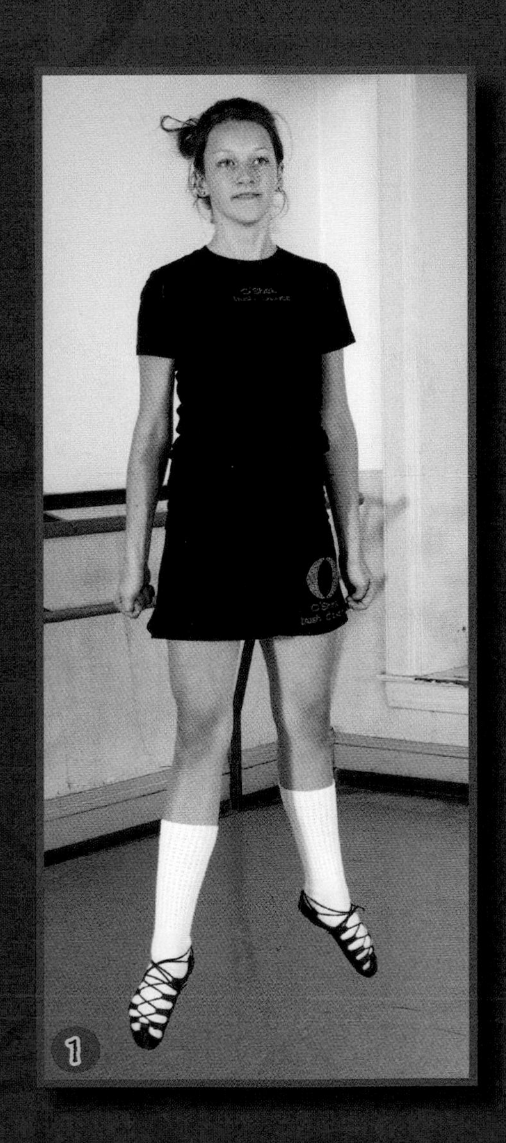
1

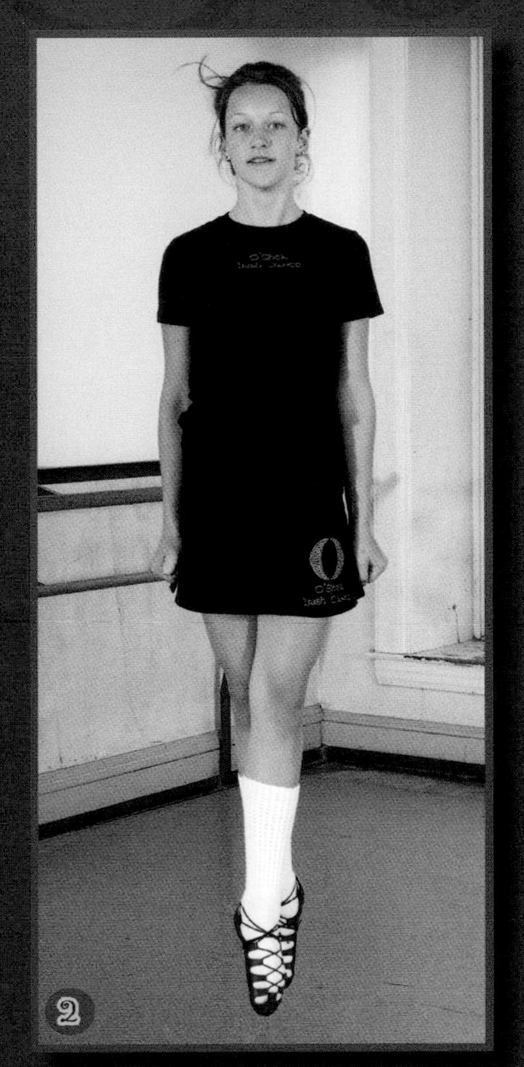
2

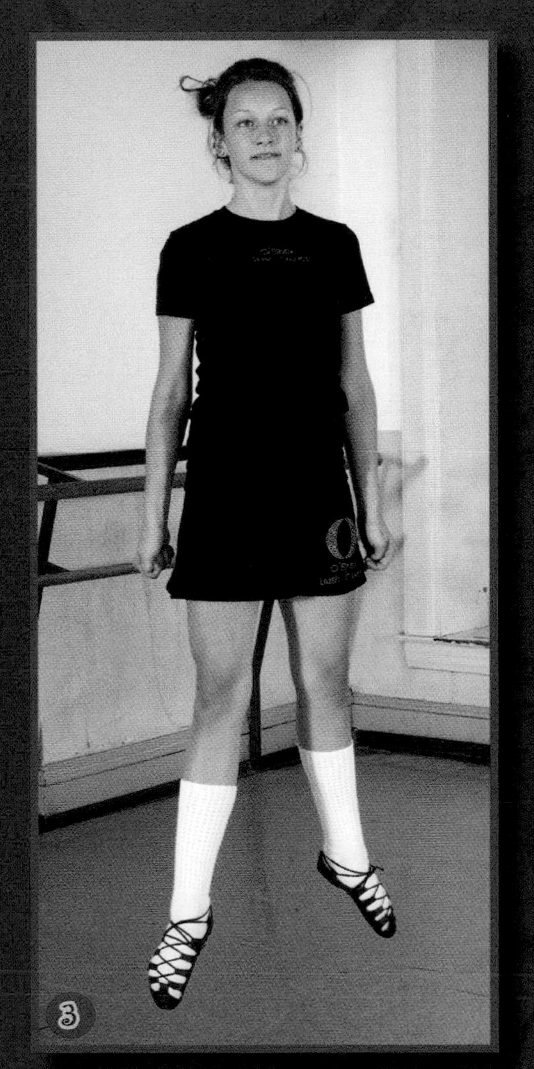
3

Chapter five

Getting Good

Ready to show off your kicks, stomps, and leaps?

In order to begin competing, you'll have to show your Irish step teacher that you can do all the required steps. Once he or she recommends you for competition, you'll head to a feis. At a feis, you can compete in different levels. Beginner levels are for the most basic dances. You'll probably start there. As you become a better dancer, you'll compete in the novice and prizewinner levels.

Regionals, or the Oireachtas (uh-ROC-tus), are the next step for Irish dance competitions. Dancers who win first place at the prizewinner level advance to the Oireachtas. The best dancers at the Oireachtas will head off to the World Championships in Ireland and the North American Championships in the United States.

2006 FEIS AT THE FAIR
OPEN CHAMPIONSHIP
SECOND PLACE
781

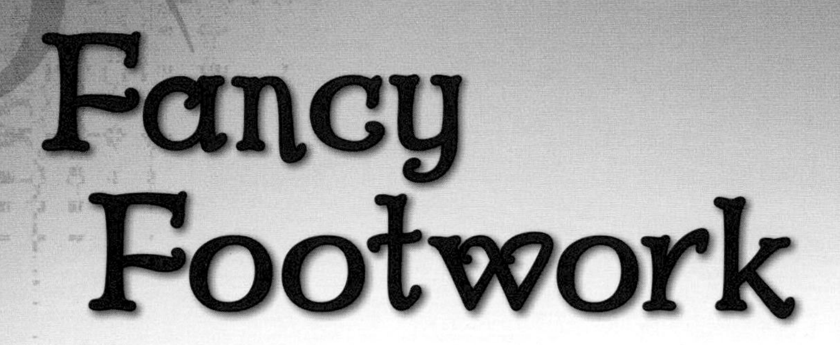

Fancy Footwork

To reach the highest levels, you'll need strong technique and fierce determination. More importantly, you'll need to practice! Top dancers practice at least three to four hours each day, five days a week.

Many competition champions move on to become professional Irish dancers. Professional dancers hit the stage in *Riverdance* and Michael Flatley's *Lord of the Dance* and *Feet of Flames*. These shows draw large audiences around the world.

But you don't need to be a serious competitor to learn Irish step dance. By practicing, performing, and having fun, you'll carry on an Irish tradition. Keep hopping and tapping those feet, and you'll have the luck of the Irish in no time!

Glossary

Celtic (KEL-tik) — belonging to an ancient group of people from western Ireland; the people were called Celts.

feis (FESH) — an Irish step dancing competition; more than one feis are called feiseanna (FESH-ah-na).

Gaels (GAYLZ) — an ancient group of people who lived in Ireland; they are also known as Celts.

ghilles (GIL-eez) — soft shoes worn by girls and women in Irish step dancing

heritage (HAIR-uh-tij) — history and traditions handed down from the past

Fast Facts

Michael Flatley created the choreography for *Riverdance*, a dancing sensation that popularized Irish step dancing all around the world. But Flatley is actually an American. He was born in Chicago, Illinois.

Before the 1930s, Irish step dancing was mostly taught to boys. But today, most Irish step students are girls.

Irish step is popular in many countries, not just Ireland and the United States. Dancers in countries like South Africa, Poland, and Taiwan are Irish stepping too.

Read More

Richardson, Hazel. *Life of the Ancient Celts.* Peoples of the Ancient World. New York: Crabtree, 2005.

Storey, Rita. *Irish Dancing and Other National Dances.* Get Dancing. North Mankato, Minn.: Sea to Sea, 2007.

Wade, Mary Dodson. *Ireland: A Question and Answer Book.* Questions and Answers. Countries. Mankato, Minn.: Capstone Press, 2007.

Internet Sites

FactHound offers a safe, fun way to find Internet sites related to this book. All of the sites on FactHound have been researched by our staff.

Here's how:

1. Visit *www.facthound.com*
2. Choose your grade level.
3. Type in this book ID **1429613513** for age-appropriate sites. You may also browse subjects by clicking on letters, or by clicking on pictures and words.
4. Click on the **Fetch It** button.

Facthound will fetch the best sites for you!

Wendy Garofoli is a freelance writer for *Dance Magazine*, *Dance Spirit*, *Dance Retailer News*, and *Cheer Biz News*. She has written other dance titles for Capstone Press, including *Dance Teams*, *Breakdancing*, *Jazz Dance*, *Swing Dancing*, and *Modern Dance*.

INDEX